LENNY & LILY
THE FLOWER SPOT KIDS

Written By Dani Liu

Illustrations By
Vidya Lalgudi Jaishankar

This book is dedicated to Lennox, Lillian,
and also you — whom we invite along to join
The Flower Spot kids crew!

"What should we do today?" Lily asked her cousin Lenny as they ran out to play. Without a second thought, Lenny shouted out, "Let's go visit our friends at The Flower Spot!"

"Yes, let's make it our own little quest!
We can put our flower knowledge to the test!"

They went into the greenhouse and were amazed by what they saw. There were flowers and plants of all colours. They stood in complete awe!

"Careful, don't touch," Lily said from behind. "The roses are pretty but have thorns that may not be so kind!

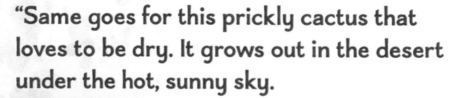

"Same goes for this prickly cactus that loves to be dry. It grows out in the desert under the hot, sunny sky.

"One of my favourites is the sunflower.
They look so happy, don't you think?
They are usually yellow, although you can
also find them in red, orange, brown and
even pink!"

"Well, I love the pumpkins," Lenny said as he ran by. "They can grow as big as a brown bear and also make a yummy pumpkin pie!

"There are tomatoes, peppers and strawberry plants too! We can grow our own little garden and have a yummy feast for both me and you!"

STRAWBERRIES

An excited Lenny and Lily ran back home with their plants, getting their little hands in the dirt and all over their pants!

They dug multiple holes in a row, then watered their garden to help all the plants grow.

All of their care, patience and love paid off in the end, as they had a colourful garden to enjoy with all of their family and friends!

First Edition: March 2022

Published by Happi Dani
www.happidani.com

Manufactured by Amazon.ca
Bolton, ON

26767511R00017